For apartment dwellers everywhere;
for Wesley, always; for Angela, forever — LH

To Logan and Oliver, who are the best
at teaching me cool things about rocks — MV

Text copyright © 2022 by Lourdes Heuer
Illustrations copyright © 2022 by Marissa Valdez

Tundra Books, an imprint of Penguin Random House Canada Young Readers,
a division of Penguin Random House of Canada Limited

Library and Archives Canada Cataloguing in Publication

Title: Esme's birthday conga line / written by Lourdes Heuer ; illustrated by Marissa Valdez.
Names: Heuer, Lourdes, author. | Valdez, Marissa, illustrator.
Identifiers: Canadiana (print) 20200410938 | Canadiana (ebook) 20200410946 |
ISBN 9780735269408 (hardcover) | ISBN 9780735269415 (EPUB)
Classification: LCC PZ7.1.H48 Es 2022 | DDC j813/.6—dc23

Published simultaneously in the United States of America by Tundra Books of Northern New York,
an imprint of Penguin Random House Canada Young Readers,
a division of Penguin Random House of Canada Limited

Library of Congress Control Number: 2020951323

Edited by Samantha Swenson
Designed by John Martz
The artwork in this book was rendered digitally in Procreate and Photoshop,
with hand-painted watercolor textures lovingly sprinkled in.
The text was set in Stratford.

Printed in China

www.penguinrandomhouse.ca

1 2 3 4 5   26 25 24 23 22

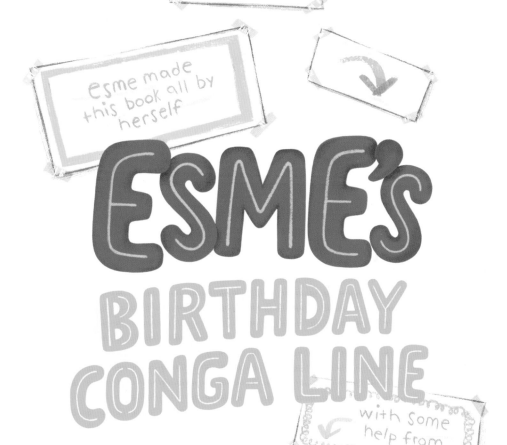

esme made this book all by herself

ESME'S
BIRTHDAY
CONGA LINE

with some help from

words by
Lourdes Heuer

pictures by
Marissa Valdez

tundra

CHAPTER 1

I live on the uppermost floor of the topmost best building!

Today is my birthday.

It is the first birthday I am celebrating since moving in with Mimi and Pipo.

"Happy Birthday, Esme!" says Mimi.

"Happy Birthday, Esmeralda!" says Pipo.

2

"Meow," says El Toro.

Mimi and Pipo place a gift in my hands.

It's a big one!

It's . . .

. . . a guitar!

"Perfecto! I can play it at my
birthday party!"

Mimi and Pipo look at each other.

They wished me a happy birthday.

They gave me a gift.

But Mimi and Pipo did not plan a party
for me, a birthday party with a pull-string
piñata, birthday cake and music!

I think, that's how it is with grandparents.

They don't know about parties or piñatas.

They don't know about birthday cake
or music.

I think, *I* can make a piñata.
I can bake a cake.
I can play music.

I can plan a party all by myself.

"Who better?" I ask El Toro,
and he agrees:

"Meow."

CHAPTER 2

All the neighbors in the topmost best building are hereby invited to my party on the uppermost floor:

- the Garcia girls

- the Mora sisters

- Mr. Leon, Mrs. Leon and Baby Leon

- and Manny, the building superintendent

Manny fixes leaks, sweeps floors and takes out garbage.

He dislikes drippy ceilings, dirty hallways and stinky things.

Mimi says, Manny dislikes elevators that
break often and children and most of all
children in elevators.

Mimi says, Manny dislikes birthdays
and parties and most of all
birthday parties.

I think, she can't mean
my birthday!
She can't mean
my party!

Who doesn't love a pull-string piñata?

Who doesn't love a piece of homemade cake and the sounds of a guitar?

Mimi says, Manny, that's who.

I hop into the elevator.

"Couldn't be!" I say.

"Going down!" I say.

"Meow."

NOT SAFE *nope*

NO CHILDREN ALLOWED

NO CHILDREN !!!

NO KIDS

DO NOT GO ON

that means you Esme!

CHAPTER 3

No one lives on the fourth floor
of the topmost best building.

For now.

I didn't always live here, and look at me
now.

The Garcia girls live on the third floor!

I saw them yesterday for one of our regularly scheduled, very important, not-to-be-missed Friday afternoon meetings.

We were just babies then!

But today is my birthday.

I think, I'm practically a grown-up now!

I tell them about the cake.

I tell them about the music.

I tell them about the pull-string piñata.

I spot ribbon on their desks.

Perfecto! If I am going to plan this party all by myself, the twins need to get started on their curlicue pull strings lickety-split!

The Garcia girls don't say a word.

They line up their blunt-tip scissors.

They break out their paper stash.

One twin holds up cardboard swatches.

One twin holds bottles of glue.

I give green cardboard the go-ahead.

I approve green glitter glue.

"More," I demand, "more!" until the piñata sparkles.

El Toro's stomach grumbles.

"Meow."

Mine, too.

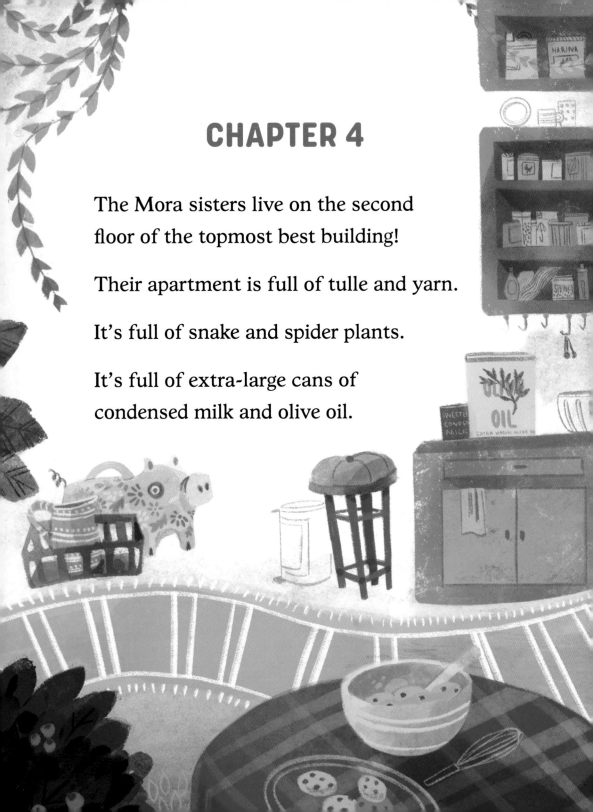

CHAPTER 4

The Mora sisters live on the second floor of the topmost best building!

Their apartment is full of tulle and yarn.

It's full of snake and spider plants.

It's full of extra-large cans of condensed milk and olive oil.

This is because the youngest Mora sister, Cari, loves to sew and knit.

The middle Mora sister, Dora, loves to plant and cultivate.

The oldest Mora sister, Lupe, loves to cook stews and bake cakes.

I think, I love to EAT cake!

I walk past Cari's dress forms.

I walk past Dora's ferns.

I walk straight into the kitchen to tell
Lupe about my cake.

Lupe listens. Lupe nods her head.

I think, Lupe gets it because she's had a *lot* of birthdays.

I tell Lupe, "Show me how you grease the pan," and she does.

I tell Lupe, "Show me how you cream the butter," and she does.

I tell Lupe, "Show me how you add the eggs and the vanilla, and how you sift the flour, and how you pour the batter and how you put it in the oven," and she does.

I close the oven door.

Perfecto! That's how I make my birthday cake all by myself!

"Meow!"

Lupe sets a timer.

"Gotta run!"

"Yes," Lupe says, "but first
we clean up, of course."

"Mmmhmm, of course!"

CHAPTER 5

Mr. Leon, Mrs. Leon and Baby Leon live on the first floor of the topmost best building!

Mimi once told me, Mr. Leon teaches music.

Mimi once told me, Mrs. Leon teaches dance.

Mimi's told me more than once that I teach everybody patience.

In their apartment, the beats are bumping.

An old record player spins.

Mr. Leon plays the bongos.

Mrs. Leon cha cha chas.

Baby Leon shakes his rattles.

I break in with my guitar.

I strum up. I strum down.

I strum up and down.

Mr. Leon pulls the needle.

Mrs. Leon freezes in place.

The baby cries with joy.

"That . . . was . . . magnifico!"
says Mr. Leon.

"That . . . was . . . bravissimo!"
says Mrs. Leon.

"Meh!" says Baby Leon in that cute way
he says my name.

I tell them about the party.

I tell them about the pull-string piñata and
the cake.

I tell them about the music I will play
with my brand-new guitar.

Mr. Leon takes it from my hands.

"No, no, no, you should not play,"
Mr. Leon says.

"No, no, you should not play,"
Mrs. Leon says.

"NO!" the baby says.

"Meow," El Toro says.

"I mean, it would be MY honor to play for YOU."

Perfecto!

If playing for me is an honor, who am I to say no?

I let Mr. Leon borrow my guitar.

I think, practice makes perfect.

CHAPTER 6

I save the best for last!

Manny, the building super, lives on the ground floor of the topmost best building.

I run into the elevator as the doors begin to close.

El Toro squeezes in behind.

But the lights don't come on.

The elevator won't move.

I think, the elevator may be broken!

"Meow."

El Toro is right.

I should inspect the elevator!

"Meow?!"

I test call buttons.

BEEP!

I adjust panels.

PLUNK!

I conduct a full examination, floor to ceiling, ceiling to floor.

BOING! BOING! BOING!

"MEOW!" El Toro says.

Inspection complete!

I straighten my glasses.

I straighten El Toro's cape.

Perfecto! The elevator starts.

"Going down!" I say.

"Meow," El Toro says.

DING! the elevator says.

"YOU!" Manny says.

CHAPTER 7

"You grounded my elevator!"

"Correct! You live on the ground floor,"
I say.

"You're last, but not least, on my list,"
I say.

"What list?"

"All the neighbors in the topmost best
building are hereby invited to my party on
the uppermost floor."

I tell Manny all about my party, my
birthday party with a pull-string piñata,
birthday cake and music.

46

I tell Manny how Mimi said he wouldn't like music, how he wouldn't like cake, how he wouldn't like things falling from pull-string piñatas.

"Couldn't be!" I say.

I hand Manny my invitation.

I hand Manny my inspection report.

I hand Manny my bill for the inspection.

I think, I smell smoke.

I think, I smell CAKE!

Time to get back to Mimi and Pipo's apartment!

But I don't trust that elevator.

I take the stairs instead.

CHAPTER 8

We stop on every floor:

- for Mr. Leon, Mrs. Leon and Baby Leon on the first floor

- for Cari, Dora and Lupe on the second floor

- and for the Garcia girls on the third

We twist our way to the uppermost floor of the topmost best building!

Mrs. Leon shakes the maracas.

Mr. Leon plays my guitar.

The Mora sisters carry the cake.

The Garcia girls bring the piñata.

El Toro brings up the rear.

His tail bobs to a beat.

"Meow, meow, meow meow meow."

One, two, cha cha cha.

One, two, cha cha cha.

Baby Leon shakes out the rhythm.

He rides strapped across Mrs. Leon's chest.

I think, that's how it is with babies.

They need all the help they can get.

CHAPTER 9

Mimi and Pipo are waiting for us.

Mr. Leon, Mrs. Leon and Baby Leon move furniture for games and dancing.

Cari decorates with streamers.

Dora arranges bouquets.

Lupe frosts the cake.

The Garcia girls take measurements.

I think, if I am going to get this party started all by myself, the twins need to hang the piñata double-quick!

I spy prizes all around Mimi and Pipo's apartment on the uppermost floor of the topmost best building.

I stuff the piñata with treasures.

The girls don't say a word.

They pack it full of stickers.

They pour in the confetti.

"More," I demand, "more!" until the piñata swells.

One twin ties the pull strings.

One twin tapes the lid.

I hand them the little ladder.

"A little more to the right."

"A little more to the left."

"A little more to the right."

"To the left . . . "

"To the right . . . "

"To the left . . . "

"Meow!"

"Perfecto!"

CHAPTER 10

It's party time!

First, we play games.

We play musical statues,
button button and hot potato.

We run three-legged,
egg and spoon,
and obstacle races.

We duck duck goose
and pop balloons
and pin the tail
on the donkey.

"MEOW!"

Then it's time for the piñata!

We stand under the doorframe.

We take hold of the strings.

"1, 2, 3 . . . "

CHAPTER 11

" . . . pull!"

Stickers and confetti drop everywhere, and prizes, everywhere prizes!

- for Lupe, two coffee spoons

- for Dora, a packet of seeds

- a handful of thimbles for Cari

- a kazoo for Mr. Leon

- and for Mrs. Leon, a ring

- Baby Leon gets a teether

- the Garcia girls, a raise

- kisses for Mimi and Pipo

- feathers for El Toro

- and for Manny, a broom
  (I swap his broken one for ours)

I think, he almost missed the party!

What took him so long?

CHAPTER 12

The party is almost over.

But wait!

We saved the best for last.

We dance our way to the table.

El Toro and I take the lead.

Baby Leon smiles.

Mrs. Leon shimmies.

Mr. Leon strums.

Mimi and Pipo keep up.

The Mora sisters keep rhythm.

The Garcia girls keep time.

Manny keeps sweeping.

I live on the uppermost floor of the
topmost best building.

Today was my birthday.

"Happy Birthday, Esme!"
say my neighbors.

"Happy Birthday, Esmeralda!"
say Mimi and Pipo.

"Meow," says El Toro.

I blow out the candles.

I make a wish.

Everyone claps.

Perfecto! Mimi and Pipo forgot to plan a birthday party for me, but I planned it easy-peasy all by myself.

I think, that's how it is with birthday parties.

Planning them is . . .

. . . a piece of cake!